TROLL HUNTERS

Troll Hunters is published by Stone Arch Books
A Capstone Imprint
1710 Roe Crest Dr.
North Mankato, Minnesota 56003
www.capstonepub.com

Summary: After they escape the underground kingdom of the trolls, the young heroes discover that their families and friends have turned against them. The teens will need aid from beyond the stars if they hope to prevail in this final battle against ancient evil.

Designed by Hilary Wacholz

Cataloging-in-Publication Data is available at the Library of Congress website.
ISBN 978-1-4342-3310-3 (library binding)

Printed in the United States of America in Stevens Point, Wisconsin.
102011
006404WZS12

WRITTEN BY MICHAEL DAHL

ILLUSTRATED BY BEN KOVAR

STONE ARCH BOOKS
www.stonearchbooks.com

TABLE OF CONTENTS

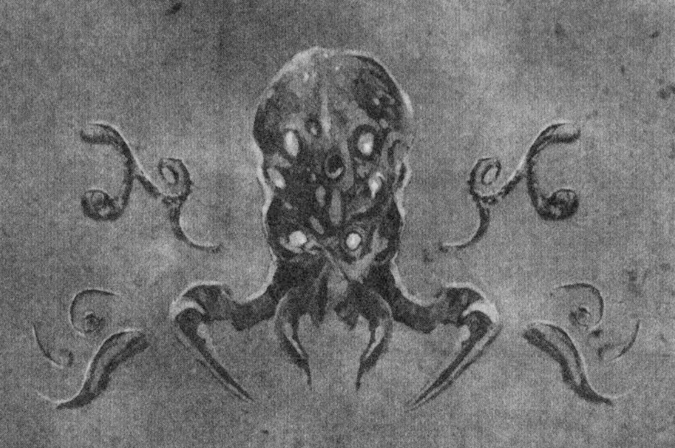

To C.S. Lewis,
Astrophile

Tonight
A star will fade and fall
Tonight
A star will flee the sky
Tonight
A star will burn to ash
Tonight
A star will die.

— from *The Last Battle* by Phoebus Glyver

APPROACHING ZION FALLS . . .

Seven-year-old Louise Tooker had seen nightmarish things over the last three nights. The big bad wolf, trolls, goblins, and creatures that spit flame like dragons. She had seen a monster that stood as tall as a tree. And she had seen another monster — a friendly one — die beneath the bad monster's foot.

Louise pinched her eyes shut, trying to shut out the pictures in her mind. But she didn't want to forget that poor creature. She knew he had sacrificed himself for them all. Without his help, they would still be trapped far below Zion Falls.

She hoped the trolls were all gone now. No more fighting. No more claws and tusks. No more friends dying.

She hoped.

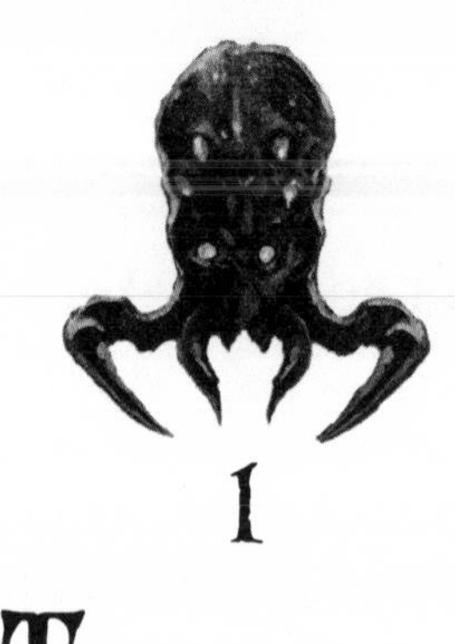

1

The Surface

East of the town of Zion Falls lay a huge abandoned quarry. The bottom of the rocky crater was filled with water, forming the biggest lake for miles around. The clear, calm waters reflected the moon and constellations overhead. Many people of Zion Falls would gather there to watch meteorite showers or gaze at the stars.

This evening, however, the lake did not reflect the heavenly bodies in the sky. The normally calm water was agitated.

An underground disturbance sent slabs of rock tumbling down the quarry's high walls. Giant boulders fell and splashed into the water. The lake trembled and stirred.

Then the lake began spiraling in one direction. A whirlpool formed with a deep, swirling hole at the center. Above the lake, lightning flashed in a clear sky. And from the center of the churning eye of the whirlpool, a golden disc rose into the air.

Shouts and cries came from the disc. On top of it was a group of humans. Their voices were loud and happy, their fists pumping in the air in celebration. The strange figure of Dr. Hoo stood above the rest, his three arms hanging from his shoulders.

"The battle has been won," said Dr. Hoo, looking down at his companions. "But the war is not over."

Zak Fisher stood up next to the doctor. "Come on, Doc," he said. "Can't we just celebrate? What happened down there was awesome!"

"Yeah!" said his friend Pablo O'Ryan, sitting by Zak's feet. "We kicked some troll butt down there!"

"It's not over yet," insisted Dr. Hoo. He walked to the center of the golden disc. "True, the *gathool* have suffered a major defeat. We struck a deadly blow to the heart of their kingdom."

"Yes!" said Zak. "I mean, did you guys see when this disc —"

The doctor held up a hand to silence Zak. "But a wounded enemy is a dangerous one," Dr. Hoo said. "More dangerous than you can imagine. Now, more than ever, we must all stick together."

Thora's gaze caught Pablo's. He looked at her from across the disc. His eyes glimmered and pulsed like distant stars.

Thora stared up at the stars. *This is where it all began,* she thought.

Three nights ago, she and her brother Bryce, along with most of the townspeople of Zion Falls, had been gathered at the water's edge in the quarry. They had come to watch the spectacular Draconid meteor shower three nights ago. All eyes were turned to the sky as the heavens above shimmered with light.

But that night, something was happening under the earth, as well. Powerful creatures, the *gathool,* known throughout history as trolls and ogres, were clawing their way back to the surface. They were hungry to enslave the human race.

On that first night, Pablo and Zak, Louise, and later Thora and Bryce, had wandered across each other's paths.

Thora . . . Thora . . .

She heard the whisper with her mind, rather than her ears. But she recognized the voice as her brother's.

Bryce lay near Thora on the floor of the golden disc. His hand reached out to hers. "Thora," he said, smiling weakly.

Bryce had been a prisoner of the trolls. His mind had been controlled by the *gathool* and filled with pain and darkness and hatred. He was slowly returning to normal now, but his body was still weakened from the recent struggles.

"You helped us down there," Thora said, smiling at her brother.

Bryce tilted his head at her. "I did?" he asked.

"Yes," Thora said. "We couldn't have defeated Ooloom without your help."

The monster's name sent a sudden jab of pain through Bryce's body. His grip tightened on Thora's hand. "It's okay," she said. "You're safe now."

Thora thought back to the fiery underground kingdom from which they had barely escaped. When she closed her eyes, she still saw giant creatures with sharp fangs and claws. And the monster known as Ooloom had been bigger than the rest. His crown of molten lava still burned in her mind.

"Is your brother feeling better?" a voice asked.

Thora turned. Mara Lovecraft was standing behind her. The wind rushed past them both, whipping their long hair into their faces. Thora nodded at the older woman.

Mara had come from somewhere far away to help them. Together, they had defeated the *gathool* three times. But this last fight had been the worst. It had nearly killed them all.

Besides the seven who had banded together to fight the trolls, the disc was transporting some of the creatures' former captives. Zak's parents were there, as were Pablo's parents. Thora's mom and dad were there too. So was Louise's father, Lionel Tooker, who had first seen the monsters when they attacked his home not far from the quarry.

Thora . . .

Thora glanced around the area.

Thora . . . Thora . . .

Is that Bryce again? Thora thought. *It sounds like him. But why is he still speaking with his mind?*

When Bryce had fallen under the trolls' dark influence, they had been able to control him. They had also been able to send his thoughts to other people. Thora thought their power over him had been broken when Ooloom died.

Zion . . . Falls . . .

"That's right," Thora said to Bryce. "We're back home."

Bryce shook his head. He looked confused.

Thora noticed that Bryce's eyes gleamed, but not like the light from the stars overhead. And it was nothing like the light she occasionally saw in her companions' eyes.

Falls . . . the whisper repeated. *Zion . . . falls . . .*

Thora felt an icy coldness grab her heart. *The voice. It isn't Bryce,* she realized.

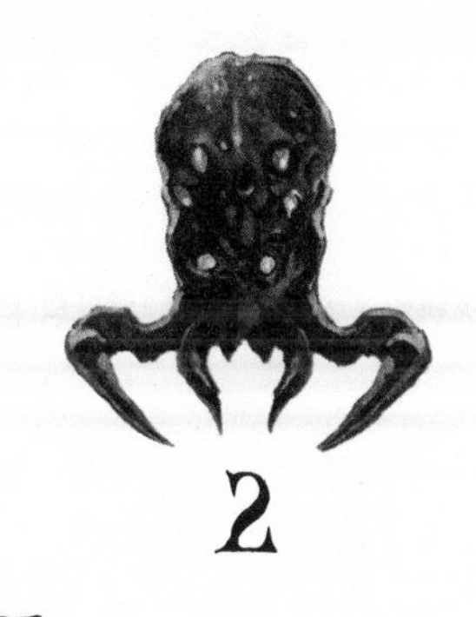

2

Unfriendly Fire

Slowly, Dr. Hoo lowered the golden disc onto the lake. The whirlpool had disappeared. The waters of the quarry were calm. As they looked down, they saw the stars glimmering in the water.

The disc settled on the surface like a golden raft. Then it floated gently in the middle of the lake. Dr. Hoo stared at the shore. The light that was reflected in his glasses seemed as red as blood. "Look," he said, pointing.

Above the western edge of the quarry, thick black smoke billowed into the sky. The bellies of the clouds there glowed an angry red.

"Is it a fire?" Thora asked.

"It's the town," said Dr. Hoo. "Zion Falls is under attack."

Zion . . . falls . . .

It wasn't only Thora who heard the whisper in her mind. The others heard it now too.

Zak Fisher's father, one of the humans rescued from the trolls, looked up at his son. "I thought you defeated them," he said.

"We outsmarted the general of the troll's army," said the doctor. "But while we were busy underground, they launched an attack up here."

"I should have thought of that," said Mara. "I've read all your books about the *gathool.* I should have known they would trick us."

"They live by deception," said the doctor. "They distracted us from the bigger battle while we were busy fighting Ooloom."

Louise shuddered at the name. "That ugly giant," she said. Her father hugged her tightly.

Pablo stood up next to the doctor. "You said this was a bigger battle?" Pablo asked.

Dr. Hoo returned his gaze to the fiery clouds swarming in the west. "Yes," he said. "Bigger because more is at stake."

Zak shook his head. "I don't get it," he said. "I thought we destroyed their entire army."

"That is true," Mara said, nodding. "But as long as their leader lives, they can always add to their army."

"Add?" repeated Pablo. "How?"

"Thora," said Bryce, staring up at her through his broken glasses. "The town . . ."

"Don't worry, Bryce," Thora said. "We'll think of something."

Pablo looked over at Bryce, who whimpered. *That's how they replace their fallen warriors,* Pablo thought. The most powerful trolls had minds that could invade human thoughts. Thora's brother had been a member of that lost army once before. An invisible force was reaching out once again to try to take hold of their minds. Pablo felt his memories and thoughts being prodded and poked.

Stick together, Pablo told himself. He tried to think about his friends. About the abandoned silo where they had fought together. They were the golden band. The four star-touched companions. Victory was possible, but only if they stayed together.

Thora's face was pinched. Pablo could tell she was trying to fight the dark thoughts too. Zak kept running his shaky fingers through his air. Louise was crying into her father's shoulder.

"Fight it, Bryce," Thora said, holding on to her brother's hand. "Fight it!"

The doctor pointed again toward the western edge of the quarry cliffs. "They are gathering," he said.

Pablo and his companions stared at the cliff edge. The rocks seemed to be moving.

No, not rocks. People. Hundreds of townspeople, friends and neighbors, who had fled from their burning homes. They stood at the very edge of the quarry, side by side, in a long line. *Like an army,* thought Pablo.

"They're really close to the edge of the cliff," said Thora. "I hope nobody falls."

Just then, the entire line of townspeople bent down. They reached their hands toward the ground. "What are they doing?" asked Louise.

Pablo's eyes went wide. *They're following orders,* he realized.

Something splashed in the water a few feet away. Louise turned her head to look. "Was that a fish?" she asked.

More and more splashes erupted around the golden disc. Then a loud bang. And another.

Definitely not fish, thought Pablo.

"Look out!" Mara shouted.

A fist-sized rock bounced off the metal disc and struck Mara's forehead. She fell to her knees and held her hands to her head. Lionel Tooker shielded Louise with his body. The other passengers huddled together, covering their heads.

A low hum began to fill the air. It grew louder, echoing through the quarry like the roar of a jet engine. Pablo's eyes went wide when he saw what was happening.

The people of Zion Falls were screaming and shouting as they threw rocks and stones.

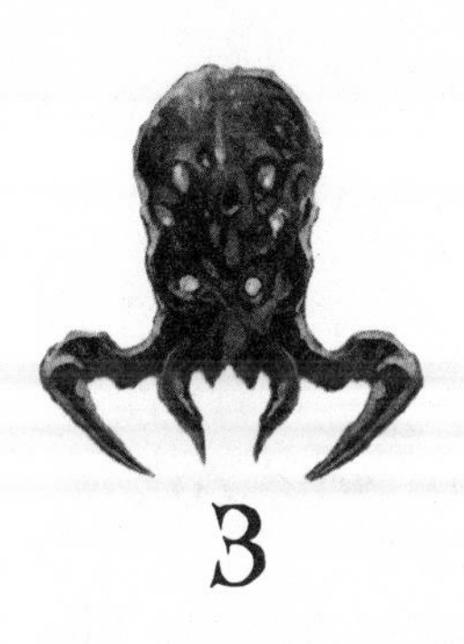

3

Engines of Destruction

"Stop it!" Pablo shouted at the townspeople. "We're your friends!"

Dr. Hoo pulled Pablo away from the edge of the disc. "The *gathool* are controlling their minds," he said. "They cannot hear you now."

Rocks rained down on them like deadly hailstones. Louise was struck on the forehead by a sharp stone.

Mr. Tooker ran to his daughter. "Louise!" he yelled.

A cut opened on Louise's forehead as she sagged into her father's arms.

"We have to get to shore!" cried Pablo.

"Swim for it!" said Zak.

The passengers on the disc leaped over and into the cold waters of the quarry. Everyone began swimming. Lionel Tooker managed to carry his moaning daughter over his shoulder as he paddled. The doctor helped Mara along with one arm while his other two slashed into the water as fast as they could.

At the edge of the quarry, the lake wasn't as deep. Everyone was wading swiftly through the water. When a few of them walked onto shore, the rocks stopped falling.

Pablo stopped where he was in the water and looked up. "They're backing away from the edge," he said.

"Are they leaving?" asked Zak.

A grinding roar burst through the air above them. A pair of lights exploded over the top of the cliff as a huge SUV zoomed off the edge of the quarry, plummeting toward the water.

"What's happening?" shouted Zak.

The SUV plunged into the lake with a violent splash.

"That's Steve Ponto's SUV," said Zak. Pablo saw that Steve and another teenager from their high school were trapped inside the vehicle. Their motionless bodies were pressed against the windshield.

Pablo turned toward Zak. "We have to save them!" he said.

"No," Mr. Tooker said. "They tried to kill us!"

Zak narrowed his eyes. "We can't just let them drown," he said.

Mr. Tooker shook his head and kept moving toward the shore. Most of the disc's passengers were already on land. Thora and the doctor were herding them to safety toward the bottom of the cliff. Only Zak and Pablo remained in the water.

"Zak!" shouted his father from the shore. "Get out of the lake!"

Pablo looked at Zak uncertainly. "He's right," Pablo said. "We need to —"

Suddenly, a loud groan pulled his attention skyward. Another pair of lights was tipping over the edge of this cliff. It seemed to be moving in slow motion. Then they saw that it was no mere SUV. This was a 60-foot-long semi truck. The axles scraped along the cliff as it teetered over the edge.

The truck boomed as it fell sideways against the rocky wall, its huge mass propelling it down toward the doctor and the others.

"Thora, look out!" Pablo yelled.

Thora and Bryce looked up to see the huge vehicle barreling down toward them. She pushed her brother to safety, falling to the ground in the process.

Thora rolled to her back and looked up to see the falling semi bearing down on her. She instinctively covered her face with her hands.

A light burst from the cliff side, pulsing outward like waves in a pool. The light wrapped itself around the semi and suspended it in midair. Thora wasted no time. She quickly crawled out from underneath the semi's shadow.

Seconds later, the vehicle crashed into the ground with a resounding, bone-shaking crunch.

Thora clambered to her feet. She was about to ask what had happened when she saw Louise hanging over her father's shoulder. The little girl's arms were straight out, light glowing from her fingertips. The light vanished and Louise went limp.

Mr. Tooker gently laid Louise against the cliff wall next to Mara. Their eyes were shut and both of them were breathing raggedly.

Zak and Pablo had been watching from the water as Louise's rings of light swept over them. They both let out a sigh of relief.

"She saved Thora!" Pablo said.

Zak nodded and smiled. "Yep — and now it's our turn," he said. He motioned for Pablo to follow him to the sinking SUV. "Let's go!"

Pablo pointed at the shouting, angry townspeople. Now they were lighting cars and SUVs on fire and pushing them over the edge.

Pablo pointed toward the shore. "We have to help your parents and the others," he said. "We have to stick together!"

Zak looked toward the cliff, then back out to the water. "You go," he said. "I'm not just leaving Steve to die."

"You idiot!" said Pablo. "Do you think you're some kind of hero or something?"

Zak grinned. "Yep," he said. "And you're my sidekick."

Pablo hesitated for only a second. "I am not a sidekick," he said.

Zak just kept grinning. "Well, are you coming?" he asked.

Pablo grunted and started swimming. Together, they swam toward the SUV.

4

DEEP WATER

The SUV floated in the water. The air trapped inside kept it from sinking too quickly, but the rear window was open a crack and water was starting to seep in. The passengers weren't moving.

"Hurry!" said Zak. He circled to the driver's side of the SUV, while Pablo stayed on the passenger side.

They both pulled on the door handles as hard as they could. The doors didn't budge.

Pablo swam behind the car and tried the side door while Zak did the same. Pablo slammed his fist against the window in frustration. "They're all locked," he said.

"Steve, wake up!" Zak yelled through the window. "Unlock the door!"

Inside the car, Steve began to stir. Blood was trickling down his face. He tried to sit up, but quickly fell back against the seat and stopped moving.

"They can't help us," said Pablo. "We need something to break the windows."

Zak smashed his fist into the window. He turned and used his elbow, ramming into the window again and again. It didn't even crack the window.

Bubbles gurgled up from under the SUV's hood as the vehicle sank deeper.

Zak and Pablo watched helplessly as the inside of the vehicle continued to fill up with water.

The cries from the angry mob traveled across the water, their voices echoing off the quarry walls. "They have us surrounded," Zak said.

The crowd was shouting and chanting together. Pablo recognized what they were saying. *Prak tara. Prak tara.* That's what the creatures had called Pablo and his friends. It meant "children of the stars" in the *gathool* language. Pablo shivered in the cold water. *Why aren't the stars helping us now?* he wondered.

"What are we going to do?" shouted Zak, his eyes darting back and forth between the crowd of people and the sinking car.

The SUV gurgled again and sank a few more inches, leaving only the roof and the tops of the windows still above water. The two boys were treading water, holding onto the door handles on the sides of the SUV. Soon, they would have to let go, or be dragged down to the bottom of the lake along with the vehicle.

Zak screamed in frustration. The scream bounced off the rocky walls surrounding them and grew in intensity. Louder and louder it grew, and deeper. It was no longer the cry of a young man. It was the growl of a ferocious bear.

"Zak!" said Pablo. "Your arm!"

Zak glanced down. His right arm had grown thicker. It was covered in fur. His nails had hardened into thick claws. His muscles bulged and expanded.

With a great roar, Zak crashed his paw into the window. The glass cracked, forming a spider web. Zak brought his bear paw back and threw a second punch, causing the window to break.

"Yes!" shouted Pablo. He swam around to Zak's side of the car and reached in to unbuckle the seat belt. Quickly, he pulled Steve through the window. Zak grabbed the other boy with his big bear paw and gently pulled him free of the vehicle.

They were just in time. With a final sickening burp, the SUV lurched forward and sank out of sight. Pablo swam back from the wake while holding on to Steve's shirt collar.

Zak and Pablo swam to the nearby golden disc, dragging the unconscious boys behind them.

As they reached the disc, the two boys half pulled, half carried the passengers onto it. Then they climbed aboard and collapsed onto their backs, panting heavily.

"Why did the trolls trap those two inside the SUV?" asked Pablo.

Zak shook his head. "I dunno," he said. He gazed down at his right arm. The fur was slowly disappearing, revealing his normal arm underneath. He flexed his fingers. "Punching that window really hurt."

"It's a good thing your powers kicked in when they did," Pablo said, turning to look behind him. "That SUV's probably at the bottom of the lake by now."

"Why didn't my whole body change?" asked Zak. "And what about you? No armor, no sword. A sword would have come in handy for breaking that glass."

Pablo frowned. "I don't know," he said.

The two boys were silent for a few seconds. They shivered in the night air, their wet clothes clinging to them.

Pablo felt weaker without Thora and Louise by his side. He looked back toward the shore. The crowd was still setting cars on fire and shoving them over the cliff's edge like flaming missiles. When each burning vehicle went airborne, the people cheered. Pablo noticed that none of the vehicles had people in them.

Maybe that's why the two passengers were locked inside that SUV, thought Pablo. *They knew we'd stay out here to help them.*

Pablo's eyes went wide. "We have to get back!" he said. "They were trying to separate us from the rest of our friends!"

Zak nodded. "You're probably right," he said. "That would explain why only my arm changed — we were too far away from the others."

Zak lay down at the edge of the disk and started paddling. Just then, a huge bubble began to rise to the water's surface from the same spot where the SUV had disappeared. Another bubble floated up, expanded, and burst. Another bubble. And another.

Pablo squinted as he looked into the water. A flat, dark object was slowly ascending toward the surface.

"What is that?" whispered Pablo.

"No idea," Zak said.

The dark object floated closer and closer. Soon, Zak recognized it. "It's the roof of the SUV!" he said.

The two watched as the broken window came into view. Then the hood and the door handles. As the SUV broke the surface, the water below the golden disc began to churn and bubble. The bobbing SUV began to rotate. The current caught the disc and dragged it in a large circle around the spinning vehicle.

Pablo froze. He wanted to jump off the disc and swim toward shore, but he was afraid of what might be lurking underneath the surface. After all, something had pushed the SUV up from the bottom of the lake. And that same something was still moving it.

Something big. Really big.

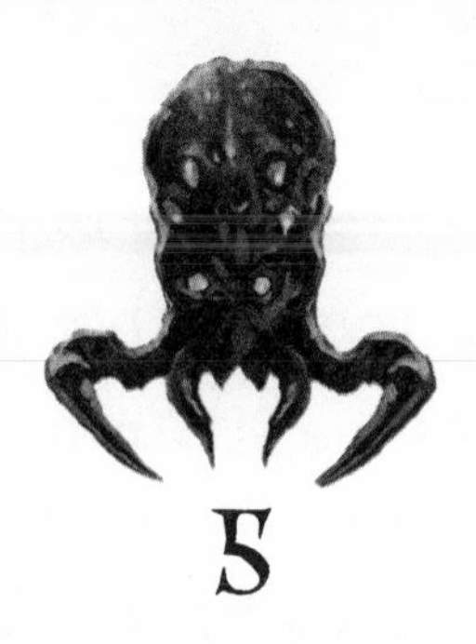

5

The Burning Wreck

Louise lay unconscious on the ground at the base of the quarry cliff. Thora bent over her. "Louise, can you hear me?" she asked.

"We have to get her to a hospital," said Louise's father.

FWOOM! Another flaming car crashed into the ground a few yards from where they all sat. Thankfully, they were all huddled beneath the base of the cliff where the rock wall slanted inward at one spot, forming a small shelter.

Thora listened to the howls of the townspeople above their heads. "I don't think we can get her to a hospital," she said.

She looked around quickly. Mara lay propped up against the cliff near Thora and the Tookers. Zak's parents were a few feet away along with the others. They were all staring at the fiery destruction raining down near them. She didn't see Dr. Hoo anywhere among them.

Thora turned to Mara. "Where did the doctor go?" Thora asked.

Mara's eyes didn't open. With an effort, she parted her lips. "You must all stick together," she said. Her voice sounded sort of strange, as if she were at the other end of a long tunnel.

"I know," said Thora. "But where is Dr. Hoo?"

Mara didn't respond. She sat motionless with her back against the cliff. She didn't seem to hear the crashes and booms from the falling vehicles.

Mr. Tooker shook his head. "She needs help," he said. "And my Louise needs help."

Thora remembered when she, Louise, Pablo, and Dr. Hoo had joined hands and healed Zak's injured hand. Maybe they could do the same for Louise now.

Thora stooped down and put her hand on Mr. Tooker's shoulder. "Let me take Louise," she said.

Mr. Tooker jerked Louise back. "What are you going to do?" he asked nervously.

"I'm going to find a doctor," said Thora. She wasn't lying. She did want to find Dr. Hoo, as well as Zak and Pablo.

"Then I'm coming with you," said Lionel.

Thora pointed at Mara. "Someone needs to stay with her," Thora said. "Don't worry. I'll come right back."

"But —" Mr. Tooker began.

Thora looked him in the eyes. "You know your daughter and I have a special connection," she said. "You've seen it." Mr. Tooker nodded reluctantly. "Then please trust me now. I'm only trying to help her."

Mara moaned. Mr. Tooker glanced at her. "All right," he said quietly.

"I'll be back as soon as I can," said Thora. She hoisted Louise up into her arms. Then she turned and ran from the cover of the cliff's edge.

Thora sprinted as fast as she could with the extra burden of Louise's weight.

But just by holding the girl, Thora felt stronger and lighter on her feet. Her path took her through a maze of burning cars and trucks. Her plan was to find the doctor, Pablo, and Zak. She knew that together they could restore Louise to health. At least, she hoped they could.

Thora wanted to put the burning cars between her and Mr. Tooker. She didn't want him to see her moving back toward the lake. He would be too frightened and confused.

She scanned the area as she ran, looking for the doctor. Where was he?

Thora kept glancing up from the smashed, fallen cars toward the top of the cliff, keeping an eye out for falling cars.

Thora . . .

Was that her brother? Thora had completely forgotten about Bryce. He was missing too.

Thora . . . I'm here . . .

Thora turned, holding Louise tight.

FWOOM! A flaming car crashed behind her, sending a wave of hot air against her back. She screamed and ran forward.

"Bryce!" she cried. "Where are you!"

Thora saw his head appear over the top of the wrecked car. His face was pale, but covered in soot. His eyes were wild and an eerie smile was frozen on his lips.

Bryce beckoned to her from the broken window. Flames danced along the edges of the car. "Here, Thora," he said. "Hide!"

"You have to get away from there!" shouted Thora. "It's dangerous."

"They're coming," Bryce said. His voice sounded like a snarling animal. "They're coming to get us."

"Bryce, you have to come with me," Thora said. "We need to find Pablo and Zak and Dr. Hoo."

Bryce saw Louise in Thora's arms. His expression clouded over. "Give me the girl!" he growled.

"What? No!" Thora said, turning Louise away from him. "We have to get her help. We have to find the others!"

Bryce pointed a finger at Louise. "Who cares about her!" he spat out. He jumped down from the car and pressed his hands to his head. He let out a terrible scream. "They're in my head! Just give her to me and they'll let me go!"

Thora shook her head. "Bryce, don't let the *gathool* control you!" she said. "You're stronger than this!"

Bryce ran toward her. He reached out and grabbed Louise's clothes, trying to yank her from Thora's grasp. Thora screamed at him, but Bryce ignored her and kept yanking. His face looked twisted and scared.

Thora pulled at Louise with all her strength. The two siblings each tugged for control of the little girl. But Thora knew that if she pulled any harder, she might harm Louise. She raised her leg and kicked Bryce square in the chest.

Bryce fell to the grown with a thud, but immediately sprang back to his feet. "I have to give her to them!" he howled, pointing at Louise. "Then they'll leave me alone!"

"No!" Thora cried.

“She must join the other one,” said Bryce. He stepped closer to Thora.

Thora tightened her grip on Louise. Bryce’s words made her legs feel weak. Despite the heat of the burning cars around them, an icy chill ran up her neck. “What other one, Bryce?” she asked, taking another step back. “Who are you talking about?”

Bryce grinned. Red light glittered in his eyes. “Who?” he said, cackling like a madman. “Who!”

Over here . . . another voice whispered.

Thora glanced around frantically. She knew that voice. As she scurried to the other side of the burning car, she saw him. Thora gasped and almost dropped Louise.

Dr. Hoo was lying on the ground next to the car. His face was gripped with pain.

As Thora knelt over him, she saw that Dr. Hoo's third arm was pinned underneath the wrecked car. He was pale. Short, shallow breaths rattled out from his throat.

"Help," he said.

6

FROM THE DEPTHS

Out in the deepest part of the lake, the SUV's tires were now visible above the surface. It continued to slowly rise from the water like a small submarine.

Zak and Pablo braced themselves, kneeling on the golden disc. They each held on to one of the unconscious boys next to them.

The SUV was completely out of the water now. Under the SUV's tires was something that looked like a small island. Black rocks and grasses sprouted from its surface.

Zak pointed a shaky finger at the island beneath the SUV. "What is that?!" he cried.

Pablo watched water steam around the island's edges. "I don't know," he said. "But it looks like it's really hot."

Hroom . . . hroom . . .

"Oh, no," Zak said, recognizing that deep, hollow booming. It was a sound they had heard in the troll's underground kingdom. The heartbeat of the giant *gathool* general, Ooloom.

"It can't be him," Pablo said. "We turned him and his entire army to stone!"

Hroom . . . hroom . . .

Pablo remembered the doctor's words. "Ooloom was merely one of the generals," Dr. Hoo had said. "Their ruler, the Great One, lies beyond."

The Great One, Pablo thought. The lord of the *gathool.* He shuddered. It was hard to imagine something worse than Ooloom.

The island rose higher and higher in the middle of the lake. It surged up like a black mountain of clay and stone and fungus. The SUV slid along the slick, wet surface. It slowly rolled down the slope of the rising island until it fell once more into the water, disappearing beneath the surface.

The island reminded Pablo of a monster's head. The rocks and grasses looked like scabs and greasy hair. The island was jet black and had disgusting spots of purplish green. It glistened with thick grease.

Then the island came to a stop. Its center was changing shape. The bumps and knobs began to spread like a fungus.

The knobs expanded and stretched in size, absorbing one another. An enormous growth was emerging in the center of the dome-shaped island.

Hroom . . . hroom . . .

The pulse throbbed louder. It shuddered through the golden disc and rattled Pablo's bones. He covered his ears with his hands, but it did no good. The sound was all around them. It was inside their heads.

Steve began to moan. His eyelids fluttered. He stared up at Zak. "Fisher?" he said. "What are you doing here?"

"Take it easy, Steve," said Zak. "We're just trying to —"

"What's that noise?" cried Steve. He turned his head. His eyes went wide with fear as he saw the pulsing island.

Pablo could not look away from the fungus-like mass. It moved as if something living was squirming under the greasy surface. The thick growth heaved upward. Lumps jutted out from the mass. Other shapes emerged, shapes that resembled arms and legs.

The mass became a fully formed creature growing out of the living island. It towered dozens of feet into the air. Four muscular arms thrust from its sides. The nightmarish creature turned its burning red eyes toward the humans.

Steve screamed. Then he passed out.

"Uzhk?" cried Pablo. The thing looked sort of like the creature who had saved them down in the *gathool* kingdom. The troll lifted his mighty arms into the air and roared angrily at Zak and Pablo.

Zak put his arm out to Pablo. "I . . . I don't think that's him," he said.

The monster howled again. His cry was answered by a howl from the surrounding walls of the crater-like quarry.

"And that's not an echo," said Pablo.

Pablo looked toward the rocky cliffs. Their rough sides were thick with long, twisting shadows. But the shadows looked too regular, too evenly spaced. Then Pablo saw the shadows move away from the cliffs.

Not shadows. Tentacles. The arms of a gigantic, squid-like monster.

Pablo realized that the dark island in the middle of the lake was merely the top of its head. The underwater beast was huge. Ooloom had seemed like a doll compared to this vast, shapeless monster.

Thool . . . ooom . . .

The creature that had sprouted at the top of the misshapen head stared at the boys. Its jawed opened and shut. Raspy sounds sputtered from its tusks. "*Prak tara,*" it bellowed. "How will that meddlesome doctor save you now?"

Zak stood up on the golden disc. "We don't need him," he said. "We'll get rid of your ugly face all by ourselves."

The monster roared. Zak met his roar with one of his own. The boy pumped his arms and screamed into the sky like a wolf howling at the moon.

Pablo stood up and moved right next to his friend. A glow began to spread up Zak and Pablo's feet and legs. It climbed up their chests and traveled across the rest of their bodies.

The silver glow now covered Zak's body. His muscles thickened and his torso expanded. Even though he still looked human, his ferocious growl sounded just like a bear's.

Pablo looked down at his feet. They were fit with shining silver sandals. His hands felt heavy. He clasped them together and saw a single gleaming sword spring into existence from the light in his palms.

He gripped the hilt in his right hand and swung it back and forth in front of him. Pablo grinned. He tightened his fingers around its hilt. It felt good to hold the Sword of Orion in his hand once again.

But something was wrong. Pablo touched his chest with his other hand.

He wasn't covered with silver armor like last time. He looked over the rest of his body and saw no armor. No helmet.

His transformation wasn't complete.

Pablo saw that Zak had grown taller and his muscles looked more powerful. But he had not transformed into the bear of his former battles, either. He was still completely human.

This was all the might that the two of them could muster alone. *We need Thora and Louise to complete our transformations,* Pablo realized. He looked at Zak and could immediately tell by the look on his face that Zak knew it too.

"Doesn't matter," said Zak. "We can take this on just like we are now."

The troll snickered. It pulled its thick feet off the island's sticky surface. They came away with a ripping sound. It extended its arm toward the sky. A gnarled bone grew out from the limb. The bone solidified into a smooth, sword-like weapon.

From behind him, Pablo heard the colossal tentacles thrashing through the waves. It looked like a single blow from one of them could wipe out an entire building. He tightened his grip on his sword. It looked puny and frail next to the monster's grand weapon. But it was, after all, the Sword of Orion. And it was all he had to defend himself — and his friend.

Zak let out a fierce battle roar. The monster lowered its weapon to its waist and lunged at them with frightening speed.

At the same time, the troll's huge sword arced through the air. Before Pablo could react, its razor-sharp tip sliced into his chest, opening a wide gash in his flesh. Pablo cried out in pain and dropped to his knees. His sword fell from his hands, clanged off the disc, and disappeared into the water.

Pablo's world went dark.

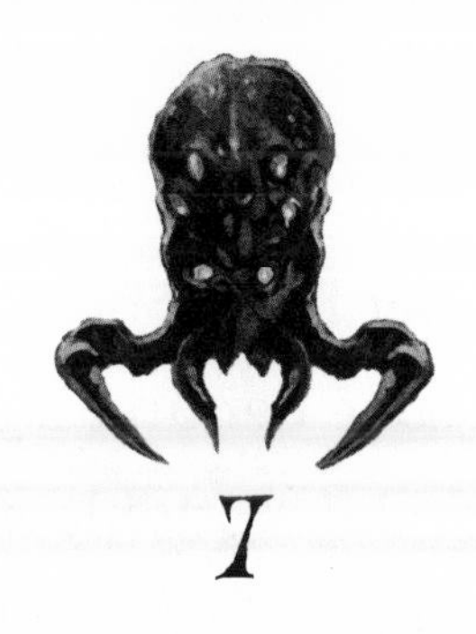

7

Blood and Water

Thora dropped to her knees next to Dr. Hoo. She ignored the burning cars, the shrieks of the townspeople, and Bryce lingering behind her. All she cared about now was the man lying on the ground before her, wracked with pain, trapped beneath a two-ton flaming wreck.

"Doctor, can you hear me?" she asked.

Dr. Hoo's eyes met hers. "You . . . you must help me," he said quietly, glancing at the limb pinned under the vehicle. "I can't move. My . . . my arm."

Thora trembled. The once-powerful doctor needed her help? She had hoped that he would save her and Louise! Thora looked down at the motionless girl in her arms. She felt like crying. She felt like giving up.

"Thora, come and hide with me," whined her brother.

"Shut up, Bryce!" Thora snapped.

The doctor reached out to her with one of his free arms. "You must help me," he said again. "I know you can."

"I can't," said Thora. She buried her face in Louise's side. "I can't." Her world was falling apart. Her brother was flipping out. Her little friend was dying in her arms. Her other friends were gone and her teacher needed her help.

"I can't do it," Thora said.

The doctor forced a smile through his pain. "The stars can," he said. He gently touched her forehead. "The ones living inside you."

A sequence of images flashed into Thora's mind as fast as she could understand them. She quickly saw the *Book of Stars* from the doctor's library. It opened. Its pages displayed a woman wearing a crown and holding a large jar. The next moment, she saw water and stars spill from the jar's mouth in a shining, silvery flood. Thora remembered the woman was Aquarius, the Water Bearer. The Mover of Floods.

Thora remembered how it felt to hold that miraculous jar in her hands. She had poured out water and stars upon her enemies as if they came from her very body.

But how can I make that jar reappear? she thought.

"The starlight," said the doctor, as if he were reading her thoughts. "Starlight is in your blood."

The doctor released his grip. He moaned with pain. He grabbed his shoulder, where the car pinned his third arm beneath a ton of glass and steel.

Thora blinked away her tears. Dr. Hoo had saved her in the woods from the first troll she had ever seen. Now it was her turn. She had to help him somehow. She had to think fast.

Thora looked down at Louise. Mr. Tooker had wrapped an old bandana around the girl's forehead to stop the bleeding. But the gash was deep. There was blood on Louise's face.

"How do I do this, Louise?" Thora asked. "Help me. What do I do?"

A gleam of silver caught her eye. Louise's blood was shining on her forehead and cheeks. Thora pulled the girl closer to her chest and closed her eyes. "Help me, Louise," she whispered.

Thora concentrated on the image of Aquarius from the doctor's book. She focused on the crown and the stars and the bottomless jar. Would they help her now? She waited for an answer, but the only sounds she heard were exploding cars and humans screaming.

Thora shivered. She looked down. Cold water was gathering around her ankles and knees. When she turned, she saw that an arm of the lake was creeping up the shore toward her.

Louise's blood glowed brighter. The water surrounding Thora grew deeper. It rose, cover her legs as she knelt next to the doctor. It washed over the doctor's chest and arms, emitting a silver light. With each wave, the pain on his face seemed to wash away.

The rushing water was carving out an inlet in the shore. It gathered up the sand and rubble and pulled them toward the lake. Thora felt herself sinking into the damp ground.

She stood up. More water flooded in from beneath her feet. The doctor disappeared beneath its foaming tide. She saw only his wet, flapping coat and one of his hands.

Then the wrecked car groaned. It began to sway. The water had loosened the ground beneath it. Thora felt a burst of energy. She raised her free hand toward the car.

Water and foam blossomed from her fingertips. The car tilted. With a long squeal, the car fell back. It crashed into the water and shot silvery spray into Thora's face.

"Dr. Hoo!" Thora cried. She looked down and reached into the rising foam. She grasped the doctor's hand and pulled it hard. The doctor rose, sputtering, through water and sand. He crawled to his knees, then stood next to her, flexing his arms. He smiled at Thora. Then his eyes went wide.

"Thora, look!" Dr. Hoo said, pointing behind her.

Thora turned. Bryce was standing in the eddying waves. The reddish gleam in his eyes glowed brighter. In his hand, he held a piece of jagged glass from a broken car window.

"Give me Louise," Bryce demanded. "They're coming! I have to give her to them!"

Dr. Hoo clenched his fists — all three of them. He moved between Bryce and Thora. "You can't trust him, Thora," Dr. Hoo said. "His mind is being manipulated."

"Give me the girl!" Bryce shouted. He raised the jagged piece of glass and made a slice through the air.

"Don't make me hurt you, Bryce," Dr. Hoo said. "Control yourself — you can do it. Just focus."

Bryce hesitated. His eyes seemed to flicker between red and blue. He shook his head left and right, as if trying to clear his mind.

Suddenly, the waves of the lake crashed and boomed behind Bryce. With a long sigh, they reared back and rose into a wall of foam. A shadowy tentacle reached out of the watery wall, wrapped itself around Bryce, and lifted him into the air.

The tentacle twitched, then pulled him underwater and out of sight.

8

CRY FOR HELP

Pablo coughed and grabbed his chest. Blood covered his hand. He had fallen onto his back on the golden disc.

Where is the Sword of Orion? Pablo thought. *And where is Zak?* His vision was hazy, but he could clearly see that only the boys they had pulled from the SUV were with him on the disc now.

Pablo glanced around quickly, searching for the Sword of Orion and his friend.

A big spray of water splashed onto the disc behind Pablo. *The tentacles,* he thought. *They're coming for us!*

But it wasn't the tentacles. It was Zak. He was climbing out of the water onto the dome-shaped island. Onto the head of the monstrous island. That creature.

"What are you doing?" Pablo shouted. Then he froze. In Zak's right hand was the Sword of Orion. Zak had dived into the cold water to retrieve it while Pablo was unconscious.

My sword looks bigger now, Pablo thought. He coughed again. The pain stabbed through his chest. More blood seeped onto his shirt. He pressed his hand tightly to the wound, but the blood still gushed out.

Zak looked at the gash on Pablo's chest. Pablo saw the familiar glimmer in his friend's eyes. Zak nodded when his gaze met Pablo's. Zak knew what he had to do without Pablo even saying a word.

Zak roared. He still had not transformed into the bear warrior, but that didn't stop him. With both hands, he raised the huge sword over his head and swung it at the fungus-like monster. The creature stepped back, narrowly avoiding the deadly blow. The Sword of Orion sank into the sticky surface of the island. Black fluid seeped out from the gash and a vast bellow trembled up from beneath the water.

Thooloom . . .

Dark waters churned and foamed around the edge of the island. The golden disc rocked as the waves lapped against it.

The fungus creature swung its weapon at Zak. He lifted his sword just in time to block the attack. The blades clanged together.

The monster attacked a second time, but again Zak deflected the blow. A rain of silver sparks shot outward from the clashing blades.

The monster swiftly tossed his sword to another of his four arms.

"Zak! Look out!" cried Pablo.

The young warrior was ready. The troll's blade sliced at Zak from a higher angle, but Zak ducked down as the troll's weapon passed harmlessly over his head.

Back and forth, their blades rang out. The Sword of Orion glowed and flickered, sending silver sparks everywhere.

Silver light temporarily lit up the scene each time Zak smashed it against the monster's weapon.

Pablo knew that Zak wasn't used to using a sword, but no one would be able to tell by watching him fight.

Zak's weapons had always been his bear talons and powerful jaws, but Pablo was amazed at how well Zak fought with a sword. It seemed that Zak's brute, bear-like strength allowed him to swing the weapon with incredible speed. The sword seemed to move on its own, pulling and twisting Zak across the vast head.

Pablo felt guilty. He had dropped the sword into the water. And if he had pushed Zak harder to leave the SUV behind, they would both be on the shore right now next to their companions.

Instead, Zak was out in the middle of the lake battling against a hideous, inhuman creature, and Pablo was slowly bleeding to death.

This is my fault, Pablo thought. *We should have all stayed together like Dr. Hoo and Mara told us to.*

The monster made a strange noise. Pablo watched as the tall creature stretched out one of his scaly arms. A second sword grew from its flexing hand.

There's no way Zak can defend himself now, Pablo thought. He tried to stand, but his legs gave out and he fell back onto the disc. *He needs my help.*

Pablo knew the four companions always had more strength when they worked together.

Together, they had healed Zak's arm after a battle with the fire trolls. Together, they had defeated the Ooloom. Alone, Zak had a fraction of his powers. He wouldn't stand a chance against that monster.

Pablo knew what to do. He took a deep breath and rolled over the side of the disc.

He took in a big breath and plunged into the lake. When his chest hit the cold water, the pain clutched his heart. For a moment, he couldn't move. He began to sink deeper into the inky lake. Far below him, he saw two red fires burning underwater. The two lights blinked at him.

Then Pablo heard the clashing of swords from above the surface. He forced his eyes open wide and clenched his teeth. He couldn't reach out his arms to swim. The injured muscles in his chest wouldn't let him.

Instead, Pablo rolled to his back and flapped his legs. As he kicked through the water, he swam up toward the edge of the island.

Pablo flapped his legs faster. When he reached the island, he dragged himself up the edge using only one arm. The other hand still gripped his wounded chest.

The fungus monster turned toward Pablo. Zak followed its gaze. When he saw Pablo lying next to him, he lowered his sword for a second. "You idiot!" Zak cried. "What are you doing here?"

"Your sidekick reporting for duty," Pablo said, struggling to grin through the horrible pain. Immediately, Pablo could tell that Zak felt stronger. Zak flexed his arms and smiled at his friend.

Then Pablo screamed.

Zak turned. The monster's twin swords were both slashing toward Pablo.

In a burst of speed, Zak dashed toward the monster. With an echoing thud, he slammed his shoulder into the creature's side and sent him reeling backward. The troll almost fell to the ground, but gathered itself at the last moment.

The fungus monster bellowed angrily and turned its gaze toward the golden disc. Pablo's eyes went wide as he turned to look. A tall, familiar figure was hovering over the disc, covered in a golden glow. As his boots touched down on the disc, Pablo saw a person cradled in each of Dr. Hoo's arms.

"Thora! Louise!" cried Pablo.

The doctor stared at the fungus monster. "Your time is up," he said. "Accept defeat, or die."

"This is just the beginning!" the creature bellowed. "It is you who must accept death!"

Then the monster roared. It lifted its arm and threw a sword at the disc with incredible speed. It flipped end over end as it flashed toward the doctor.

The doctor shifted his weight and dropped Thora and Louise onto the disc. A split second later, the monster's sword sliced off Dr. Hoo's third arm at the elbow. He collapsed on the disc. Thora screamed.

Zak's eyes went wide as the beast raised the other sword, preparing to finish the job.

"No!" shouted Zak. He swung the Sword of Orion at the beast and knocked the sword from its hand. The monster's eyes shifted to Zak.

The troll immediately lunged sideways at Zak. Its massive jaws opened wider than Pablo thought possible.

With a sickening crunch, the monster's jaw clamped onto Zak's torso and lifted him off his feet.

Zak and Pablo both cried out at the same time. The monster lifted Zak high overhead, shaking his bleeding body like a rabid dog.

"Zak!" shouted Pablo.

"No!" Thora shouted.

A horrible sound came from the monster's jaws as Zak's bones snapped. He went limp.

But Zak somehow managed to hold on to the Sword of Orion. With his remaining strength, Zak plunged the blade into the monster's head — all the way up to the hilt.

Zak released the sword and went limp. The troll dropped him, and he fell in a heap onto the island. The monster stumbled, retching and coughing. It tried to pull out the sword, but it couldn't reach the blade.

The island heaved and jerked underneath. Pablo saw that the monster was attached to the island by a long cord. As the troll thrashed and writhed, its pain was shared by that creature below the water.

Finally, the monster grasped the sword. As its fingers wrapped around the hilt, its hand began to crack and crumble. Three arms fell to pieces like shattered pottery. In seconds, the creature had crumbled into a mass of dirt and clay and stone upon the island. In the middle of the pile laid the Sword of Orion, glinting in the moonlight.

The island thrashed wildly, threatening to knock Pablo off. He knew he would face those burning eyes again under the waves. And those fearsome tentacles. *A wounded enemy is a dangerous one,* Pablo remembered.

Pablo crawled over to the fallen sword. He tilted the sword and shifted his weight onto it, then he used it to climb to his knees.

He raised the Sword of Orion over his head. With every ounce of strength he had left, he brought the sword down, plunging it into the center of the island.

A hideous shriek rose up from beneath the water. The island shuddered. Its long tentacles curled up and surged toward Pablo.

Thora and Louise suddenly appeared at Pablo's side. Kneeling, they placed their hands on top of Pablo's.

A ball of shimmering light grew around their hands. Lights twinkled in the water around them. The stars overhead were motionless, but the reflections on the waves quivered and stirred.

The island shook violently. "Hold on!" yelled Thora.

The star reflections whirled around them like a blizzard of fireflies. The light from the sword grew more intense as the lights danced around it.

Like moths to a flame, Pablo thought.

Suddenly, the starry lights all flew toward the center of the island. The stars rushed toward the sword and passed through the companions' hands. Light dived down the length of the blade and into the creature below. The sword hilt blazed like the sun.

Thora reached out and grasped Zak's limp hand. The light grew brighter, and an explosion rocked the quarry. The surprised cries of the townspeople carried across the lake.

Slowly, the starry light faded. Small cracks ran along the island's surface. When Pablo reached his hand down to touch the island, he felt that it had turned to stone.

"Did we do it?" whispered Thora. Pablo looked over the edge of the island. The burning eyes from below had vanished.

Dr. Hoo looked at Thora and nodded. He looked relieved, despite his missing arm. "Thooloom was the father — the creator — of the *gathool* species," he said, a faint smile on his lips. "They are born from his body, created in his image. With him dead, and their army destroyed, the war is over."

Pablo felt the cold, hard stone beneath his hands. He traced a finger along the jagged cracks that ran along the petrified troll's head. "So, he's dead?" Pablo asked. "For good?"

Dr. Hoo nodded. "For good," he said. "The world is safe now. Because of you."

Thora sank to the ground, relieved. Pablo smiled.

But his smile faded when he heard Louise crying. She was leaning over Zak, tears streaming down her face.

Pablo crawled across the sticky clay toward them. He shook Zak's shoulder. "Zak, wake up," he said. "It's over now."

Zak didn't move. Blood streamed from a dozen wounds in the boy's torso and arms. Then his eyes fluttered, opening halfway.

"Zak!" yelled Pablo.

Zak smiled weakly. "Pablo?" he asked, in a raspy voice. His eyes gleamed with strange unearthly light that Pablo had seen many times before.

Pablo grinned. "Yeah, it's your sidekick," he said. "I'm right here."

Thora and Louise bent down next to Pablo. Behind them, Dr. Hoo stood silently.

"We're all here," said Thora.

"We'll take you home," said Louise.

Zak coughed. His body trembled. The starlight flickered in his eyes. "You're the best friends . . . anyone could ever have." he said. He blinked his eyes once, twice, then closed them for the last time.

9

A NEW STAR

Pablo felt a hand turn his body over. A dark shadow loomed over him. He heard the splash of water nearby.

"You passed out," said Thora. "We brought everyone here."

Pablo rolled onto his side. He was lying on the far eastern shore of the quarry lake.

Red clouds from the smoking town hung above the western cliffs. A mass of burning cars littered the opposite shore.

"Zak!" Pablo cried, remembering what had happened. "Where's Zak?"

"Stay still," Thora said. "You've been through a lot."

Pablo clutched at his chest. It still ached a little, but the wound was gone. He saw Louise sitting next to Thora. A few feet away, the doctor was kneeling over Zak's motionless body.

"Is he okay?" asked Pablo.

Thora's eyes were filled with tears. "We were able to heal your wound," she said. "And Louise's head, too."

"The doctor lost an arm," Louise said.

Dr. Hoo smiled down at her. "I'll be fine," he said.

Pablo sat up a little higher. "Is Zak all right?" he asked, his voice trembling.

Dr. Hoo didn't respond. He kneeled over Zak. Pablo couldn't tell, but it looked like the doctor was crying.

Thora shook her head sadly. "We tried," she said to Pablo. "We tried really, really hard."

Pablo hung his head. For a few moments, no one spoke.

Louise tugged at Thora's arm. "Tell him about Mara," she said.

"Mara's . . . gone?" asked Pablo.

Thora shook her head. "She's not dead," she said. "She left Zion Falls. The doctor said she finished what she came to do."

"Well, where is Mara now?" Pablo asked.

Louise pointed to the stars above the quarry. "She's up there," the little girl said. "With her sisters. The stars."

Thora turned toward Dr. Hoo. "Then Mara used to be one of us?" asked Thora. "Like it says in the *Book of Stars*?"

The doctor turned around slowly. His face was pale and gaunt. "Yes, Thora," he said quietly. "Like in the *Book of Stars*. And tonight, the book will have a new page."

Pablo gazed at his fallen friend. His lips trembled.

Dr. Hoo placed a hand on Pablo's shoulder. "He was a true warrior," Dr. Hoo said. "The mighty Arcturus. The Great Bear."

"But we're all together now!" Pablo said. "We can join hands — join our powers, like we did before. We can bring Zak back!" He looked left and right at his friends, then at Dr. Hoo. "Can't we?!"

Dr. Hoo frowned. "There are some things even the stars can't do," he said.

"No!" shouted Pablo. "But Zak . . ." A sob burst up from his throat.

"Zak sacrificed himself for his friends," said the doctor. "That is the last — and greatest act — a warrior can do."

"I would rather have died for him," Pablo whispered.

"Me too," said Louise. Thora nodded, tears streaming from her eyes.

Dr. Hoo smiled faintly. "And that's why the four of you were chosen by the stars," he said.

Pablo walked over to Zak's body. He knelt down next to Dr. Hoo. Thora and Louise knelt next to him. Pablo couldn't speak.

Louise reached out a hand and placed it gently upon Zak's chest. "Brave, big bear," said Louise. "We'll never forget him."

Thora nodded. "Never, Louise," she said.

Dr. Hoo put his arms around their shoulders. "Zak's time on Earth is finished," he said. "But he will never be forgotten. It's time for him to take his place among the stars."

Dr. Hoo placed his left hand on Zak's chest. He closed his eyes and concentrated.

The friends watched in awe as a silver light slowly began to glow beneath the doctor's palm.

The light seemed to come from deep within Zak's body. Its tendrils wrapped around the doctor's hand, swirling in his palm like a dancing light.

The doctor stood and raised his arm. The light rocketed from his hand, shot into the sky.

"Farewell, Arcturus," said the doctor.

Pablo took the hands of Thora and Louise. All of them watched as a single star blinked into existence above Zion Falls, joining its ancient companions in the heavens.

EPILOGUE

THREE WEEKS LATER . . .

Snow dusted County Road One where a rusty school bus squealed to a stop. Two girls climbed off together. It was not their regular stop. Bundled up tightly in coats, scarves and gloves, they made their way up a rough dirt driveway. The tree branches overhead were bare. The wind was bitterly cold.

At the end of the long driveway stood a huge stone house. At the top of a stone tower, dark windows, like empty eyes, stared across the winter fields. "Dr. Hoo," called out Louise as she and Thora stepped inside.

They called again. There was no answer.

They climbed to the doctor's library at the top of the tower. The room was still charred from the fire trolls. Books and shelves lay scattered across the blackened floor.

Thora was quiet. After the last month, after the terrible battles, after losing her brother and her friend in one nightmarish night, she couldn't bear it if the doctor was gone, too. "Where did he go?" asked Louise.

Something crackled behind them. The girls turned and stared at a book lying on the floor. "The *Book of Stars*!" shouted Louise.

The large volume lay open. Its pages shuffled back and forth, as if moved by invisible hands. The two girls edged closer, carefully watching its moving pages.

"Why is it doing that?" asked Louise.

Thora stared at the colorful pages. Stars and constellations whirled past. Names and shapes she had never seen before. "I think," she said with a smile, "that the book is looking for more heroes."

ABOUT THE AUTHOR

As a boy, MICHAEL DAHL persuaded his friends to celebrate the Norse gods associated with the days of the week. (Thursday was Thor's Day, his favorite!) Dahl has written the popular Library of Doom series, the Dragonblood books, and the Finnegan Zwake series. As a Norwegian lad from the Midwest, he believes in trolls.

ABOUT THE ILLUSTRATOR

BEN KOVAR was born in London. He trained in film and animation and spent several years as an animator and art director before moving into writing and illustrating fiction. He lives in an attic, likes moisture, and has a fear of sunlight and small children.

Notes on the Prak Tara

"Once every generation, the gathool rise to the surface to reclaim the world for themselves. And once every generation, the stars fall from the heavens to lend their powers to the *prak tara*. Otherwise, humankind would have no way to stop the invasion."

— from *The Celestial Cycle* by Phoebus Glyver

Dr. Glyver was the first to suggest that the powers given to the *prak tara*, or the bearers of light, come from constellations. I can confirm that this is true, as I have seen the stars choose human warriors first-hand. The scope of the *prak tara's* powers are limited only by their imaginations. The celestial powers bring out the strongest parts of each individual. Additionally, the closer the *prak tara* are to each other, the stronger they become. Seeing Zak, Louise, Thora, and Pablo combine their might was the most awe-inspiring thing I've ever seen.

I do not pretend to understand how the stars decide which four humans to choose. But from my experiences with this generation's *prak tara*, there is no question that the constellations pick wisely.

It has been my life's honor to help Thora, Pablo, Louise, and Zak unite together and harness their powers. If it weren't for them, I would be dead... and so would you.

The Gathool Vocabulary

The gathool language doesn't have many words, and the pronunciation is usually straightforward. However, many gathool words have several meanings, so translating the language is quite a challenge. Here are some of the words I've managed to decipher...

HROOM (har-OOM)—there is no standard definition for this word. It sounds like a drum, and serves as a rally cry for troll leaders.

OOLOOM (oo-LOOM)—harvester of souls. Ooloom is an honorary title given to the leader of the troll army. Only Thooloom, also known as The Great One, commands more power and respect.

PRAK TARA (PROK TAR-uh)—the bearers of light. The phrase refers to the four humans fated to oppose the trolls in a grand battle.

THOOLOOM (thoo-LOOM)—the Great One. They say he has surfaced only once before — thousands of years ago — causing a cataclysmic effect that wiped out nearly all life on the surface. If unopposed, his presence means just one thing: the skies will be filled with darkness, snuffing out the light from the stars above for centuries to come.

Benjamin K. Hoo

Find websites and more books like this one at facthound.com.
Just type in the book ID: 9781434233103